The Midnight Farm

Reeve Lindbergh

The Midnight Farm

paintings by Susan Jeffers

A Puffin Pied Piper

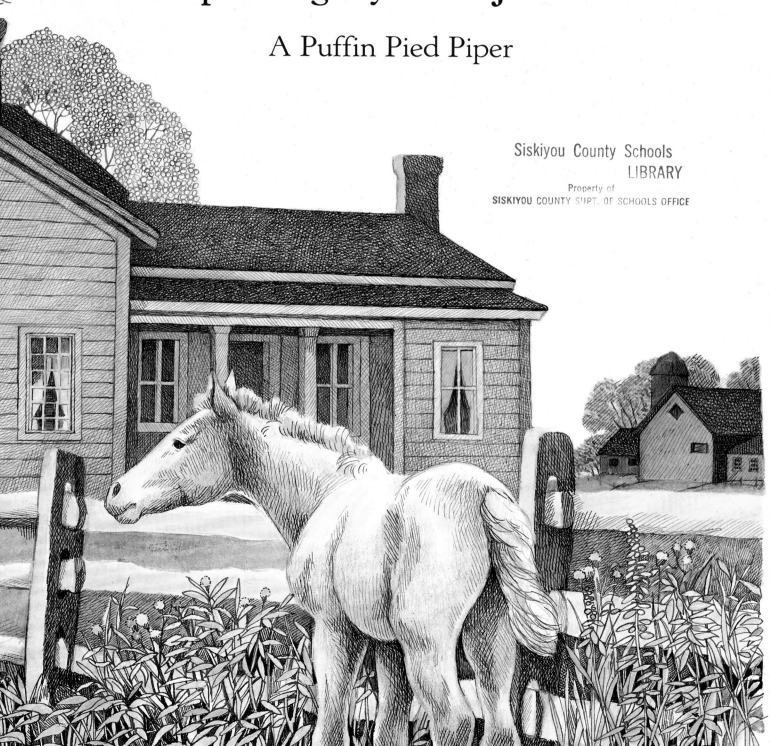

For Jonny and for Jane, with love
R. L.

For Uncle Ralph and Aunt Claire
S. J.

PUFFIN PIED PIPER BOOKS
Published by the Penguin Group
Penguin Books USA Inc., 375 Hudson Street, New York, New York, 10014, U.S.A.
Penguin Books Ltd, 27 Wrights Lane, London W8 5TZ, England
Penguin Books Australia Ltd, Ringwood, Victoria, Australia
Penguin Books Canada Ltd, 10 Alcorn Avenue, Toronto, Ontario, Canada M4V 3B2
Penguin Books (N.Z.) Ltd, 182–190 Wairau Road, Auckland 10, New Zealand
Penguin Books Ltd, Registered Offices: Harmondsworth, Middlesex, England
Originally published in hardcover by
Dial Books for Young Readers
A Division of Penguin Books USA Inc.

The full-color artwork was prepared using a fine-line pen
with ink, dyes, and gouache. They were applied over a detailed
pencil drawing that was then erased.

THE MIDNIGHT FARM
is also available in hardcover from
Dial Books for Young Readers.

Here is the dark when day is done,
Here is the dark with no moon or sun,
Here is the dark when all lights are out,
Here is the heart of the dark.

Here is the dark of the chair in the hall
Where one old dog curls up in a ball,

Breathing each breath with a rise and a fall
In the dark of the chair in the hall.

Here is the dark by the big wood stove
Where two white cats have a leftover glove

And a birthday card that was signed with love
In the dark by the big wood stove.

Here is the dark of the maple tree
Where a raccoon family, one, two, three,

Is making a home in a place that was free
In the dark of the maple tree.

Here is the dark by the barnyard gate
Where four farm geese are staying up late.

They know wild geese will come if they wait
In the dark by the barnyard gate.

Here is the dark of the stable door
Where five horses stamp their feet on the floor

And blow through their noses and stamp some more
In the dark of the stable door.

Here is the dark in the barn at night
Where six cows stand, all black and white.

Their heads are low and their eyes are bright
In the dark in the barn at night.

Here is the dark in back of the barn
Where seven fat sheep are keeping warm

On hay from the meadows surrounding the farm
In the dark in back of the barn.

Here is the dark where the chickens rest
Where eight little chicks have feathery breasts

And ruffled up shoulders and heads on their chests
In the dark where the chickens rest.

Here is the dark of the orchard pond
Where nine deer gather from all around

To drink at night without any sound
In the dark of the orchard pond.

Here is the dark of the old stone wall
Where ten small field mice scamper and call

While hiding the seeds and berries that fall
In the dark of the old stone wall.

Here is the dark of the midnight farm,
Safe and still and full and warm,

Deep in the dark and free from harm
In the dark of the midnight farm.

Susan Jeffers

is the celebrated illustrator of *Brother Eagle, Sister Sky: A Message from Chief Seattle* (Dial), which was a *New York Times* Best Seller, winner of the 1992 ABBY Award (the American Booksellers Association's Book of the Year), and *Parents* Magazine's Best Children's Book of 1991. She was a Caldecott Honor artist for *Three Jovial Huntsmen,* which also received the Golden Apple Award at the Biennale of Illustrations in Bratislava. Ms. Jeffers's other books for Dial include Reeve Lindbergh's *Benjamin's Barn,* a *Redbook* Best Children's Picture-book of the Year; Longfellow's *Hiawatha,* a *School Library Journal* Best Book of the Year; and four fairy tales retold by Amy Ehrlich: *Cinderella, Thumbelina, The Wild Swans,* and *The Snow Queen,* each an *American Bookseller* Pick of the Lists, among other honors. Ms. Jeffers lives in Croton-on-Hudson, New York.

Reeve Lindbergh

is the daughter of Charles *(The Spirit of St. Louis)* and Anne Morrow Lindbergh. *The Midnight Farm* was her first children's book, originally published in 1987 by Dial Books for Young Readers. Other books for Dial include *The Day the Goose Got Loose,* illustrated by Steven Kellogg, and her most recent book, *There's a Cow in the Road,* illustrated by Tracey Campbell Pearson. *The Midnight Farm* was inspired by her oldest daughter, who was afraid of the dark when she was very young. Ms. Lindbergh writes, "I used to tell her stories about the farm where we lived, making the nighttime darkness less frightening, I hope, by describing the animals and their activities at night in as warm and comforting a way as possible." Ms. Lindbergh lives in St. Johnsbury, Vermont.